W9-CAE-074

M.F.K.

M.F.K.

NILAH MAGRUDER

San Rafael, California

RING!
RING!
RING!
RING!
RING!

OMAR! GET INSIDE THIS MINUTE!
MY EYE!

THE FORELEVER IS SPINNIN' AGAIN!
GIVE IT ANOTHER CINCH, JAIME.
FWMP!
NO, CLOCKWISE, BOY! CLOCKWISE!
HOW MANY TIMES I HAVETA TELL YA--

...
JAIME?
WHAM!
OW!
WHAT WAS THAT FOR?!
HEH HEEH.
THAT'LL GET YA FOR IGNORIN' ME.

THAT WAS A COMPLETELY UNREASONABLE REACTION!
YOU COULD'VE GIVEN ME ANOTHER CONCUSSION!
I KNOW! WHY D'YA THINK I DID IT?
MAYBE IF I HIT YA HARD ENOUGH I'LL TURN YER BRAIN UPSIDE DOWN AND END UP WITH A GRAND-SON WHO'S ACTUALLY USEFUL!
JEEZ, YOU'RE GRUMPY TODAY.
WHY ARE WE EVEN OUT HERE? I TOLD YOU THERE'D BE A SANDSTORM!
AND WHEN D'YA THINK THE BEST TIME TO GATHER SAND IS, YA GREAT MOTHBRAIN?!
NOW CHECK THE SPIDER TRAP. MAKE SURE IT AIN'T CLOGGED.

BURP

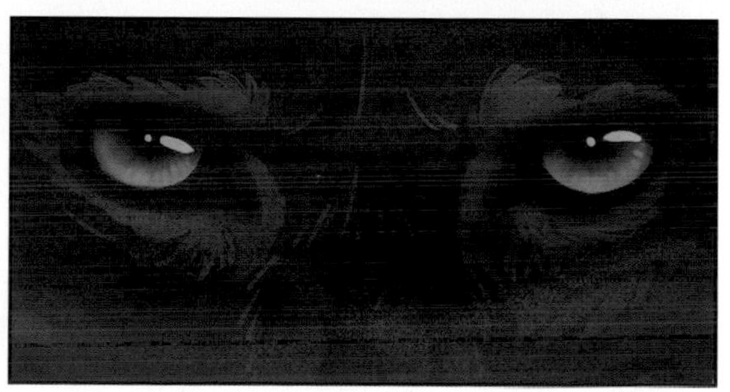

HEY,
GRAMP.

A BIT SULFURY.
THIS WIND MUST BE BLOWIN' IN ALL THE WAY FROM THE SPINE.
STORM'S TAKIN' A TURN. WE BETTER--
LOOK.
WHEEZE
WHEEZE

C'MON.

KREEEEEEE
HOOOKRKOOE
OOOOOKR
GO AWAY!
KREEOOOOOO
YOUR MOA'S HURT.
KRK...
KRR...
!
SO ARE YOU.
WHAT ARE YOU, DEAF? GO AWAY!
NO! I'M... I'M NOT DEAF!

JAIME!
TH' HELL'RE YOU DOIN', CHATTIN' HER UP?!
IT'S A FUGGIN' SANDSTORM!
SHE TOLD ME TO GO AWAY!
AW, AIN'T THAT NICE? GET 'ER UP, LET'S GET GOIN'!
STOP!
IT'S NOT GONNA MAKE IT!
I HAVE TO
HELP...
KOOOFEE
GOTTA LEAVE IT, KID!
I HAVE TO--
I
HAVE
TO

SHHK!

JAIME!

Abbie.

CLICK
ME NOW, CAN'T YOU?
IT WAS PRETTY BUSTED UP. I PUSHED THE WIRES BACK IN AND PATCHED IT AS BEST I COULD.
INTERESTING BIT OF GADGETRY. SOMEONE MAKE IT FOR YOU?
WHERE... AM I?
WELCOME TO LITTLE MARIGOLD, THE SANDIEST TOWNLET THIS SIDE OF THE NECK.
YOU'RE LUCKY MY NEPHEW FOUND YOU.

DEHYDRATED...
QUITE A BIT OF BLOOD LOSS. BUT THE DANGER'S PAST NOW.
NOT ANOTHER MOVE!
BUT I...
I KNOW YOU COULDN'T TELL BECAUSE OF THE STORM.
BUT THERE'S NOTHING AROUND HERE FOR MILES.
YOU'RE HURT.
AND YOUR MOA'S DEAD.
...
HOW FAR DO YOU THINK YOU'LL GET?
OH HEY, YOU'RE AWAKE!

SUPPER IS SERVED!
CAREFUL WITH THAT, JAIM--
SPLAT
IT'S PIGEON SOUP. DOCTOR'S ORDERS.
I MADE IT MYSELF.
HOW IS IT?
YES, IS IT EDIBLE THIS TIME?
HEY, I FOLLOWED YOUR RECIPE EXACTLY!

SO, WHATCHA THINK?
SLIDE
EHHH. I MAY NOT'A CUT UP THE PIGEON ENOUGH.
ALL RIGHT, LAD, LEAVE OFF TRYIN' TA KILL YER AUNT'S PATIENT JUST AFTER SHE PATCHES HER UP.
BUT 'M NOT...
HOW YA FEELIN', GIRL?
STILL SHAKEN UP, HUH? DON'T WORRY.

THURR'S MY YOUNGEST, NIFRAIN.
SHE'S A DOC, SO YER IN GOOD HANDS.
AND THURR OAF'S MY GRANDSON, JAIME.
HE'S HARMLESS, MOSTLY.
PFF
LOVE YOU, TOO, GRAMPS.
SO...
WHAT'S YOUR NAME?
S'ALL RIGHT, KIDDO. Y'AINT GOT NOTHIN' TO BE AFRAID OF--
BOOOOOOOOOOMMMMMMM
RATTLE
WHAT THE FUGGIN' BALLS WAS THAT?!
RATTLE
RATTLE

DING DING!
DING DING
DING DING!
BOOOM
FZZZZT!
THIS AGAIN.
DING DING!
DING DING!
FZZZSH!
KRRSSHHHH
HEH! THOUGHT THINGS WERE GETTIN' A BIT QUIET AROUND HERE.
ALMOST BEEN A MONTH. INNIT?
THIS SHOULD DO IT.
HURRY UP. YOU AND DAD GET GOING.
I GOT A PATIENT TO SEE TO.
WON'T THE MAYOR BE TICKED IF WE'RE NOT ALL OUT THERE?

IF HE'S GOT A PROBLEM WITH IT...
HE'S WELCOME TO COME BY AND TELL ME HIMSELF.
SCARY AS ALWAYS, AUNTIE.
GOOD LUCK-- YOU'RE GONNA NEED IT!
THWAP!
QUIT SCARIN' THE POOR GIRL.
OW!
JEEZ, GRAMPS!
GET SOME REST.
DON'T WORRY, IT SOUNDS WAY WORSE THAN IT IS.
BUT WHAT IS--
ARE YOU STILL HARD OF HEARING?
I SAID REST!
RIGHT NOW, DAMMIT!

TNK
HFFF
CLICK
BOOM
BOOM
BOOM
BOOOOOM
BOOM
BOOM
BOOM
BOOM

Girl,
I burned
all your
clothes.
~Nifrain
(the doctor)

THIS STUFF DOESN'T EVEN MATCH...

CRKK...

CREEEAK

TWUNK!

UH...
SORRY...
I DIDN'T EXPECT...
ERR...
Y'WANT SOME ICE?
YETH.
YETH. I DINK DAT'D BE BETHT.
ICE
UNNGGHHH...
ICE
WHAT WERE YOU EVEN DOING, ANYWAY?
UH...

I WAS JUST... UM...
YOUR AUNT GAVE ME CLOTHES, SO I WAS...
THINKING...
AND THEN... I...
BORED, HUH?
COME WITH ME.
ICE

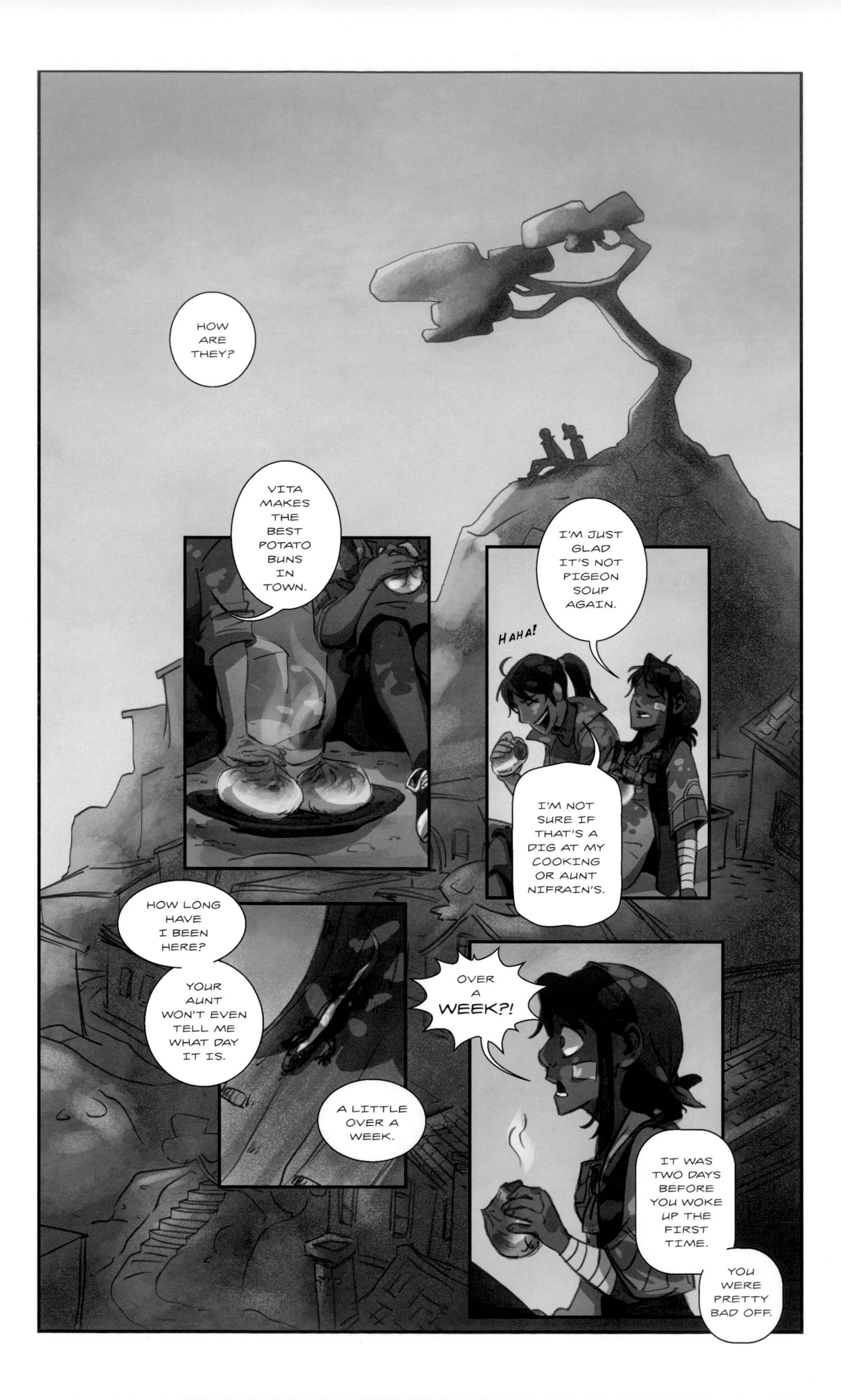
HOW ARE THEY?
VITA MAKES THE BEST POTATO BUNS IN TOWN.
I'M JUST GLAD IT'S NOT PIGEON SOUP AGAIN.
HAHA!
I'M NOT SURE IF THAT'S A DIG AT MY COOKING OR AUNT NIFRAIN'S.
HOW LONG HAVE I BEEN HERE?
YOUR AUNT WON'T EVEN TELL ME WHAT DAY IT IS.
A LITTLE OVER A WEEK.
OVER A WEEK?!
IT WAS TWO DAYS BEFORE YOU WOKE UP THE FIRST TIME.
YOU WERE PRETTY BAD OFF.

BUT IT LOOKS LIKE YOU'RE DOING LOADS BETTER NOW.
OUT OF BED AND ALL.
ONLY BECAUSE THAT WOMAN WASN'T AROUND.
SHE HASN'T LET ME MOVE SINCE I GOT HERE.
"SO THIS HAPPENED..."
WHERE ARE YOU GOING?
N...NOWHERE...
WHERE ARE YOU GOING ?!?!
JUST... NEEDED SOME AIR...
WHERE ARE YOU GOING ?!?!
TO THE BATHROOM!
IS THAT A PROBLEM?!
WUNK!

SHE ACTS LIKE I'M PLANNING A CRIME SPREE.
HEH. DON'T TAKE IT PERSONALLY.
IT MEANS SHE CARES ABOUT YOUR WELL-BEING!
OR SHE'S TRYING TO BORE ME TO DEATH.
HAHA! YEAH. SHE'S SCARY...
BUT A GOOD DOCTOR.
"DUNNO HOW THIS TOWN'D MAKE IT WITHOUT HER."
WHY'S THERE BLOOD IN MY ICE BOX?!
I DIDN'T EVEN KNOW THERE WAS A TOWN OUT HERE.
WELL, IT'S PRETTY TINY.
BET IT'S NOT EVEN ON MOST MAPS.
ISN'T IT HARD?
YOU'RE COMPLETELY ALONE OUT HERE.
WE WEREN'T ALWAYS.
THERE USED TO BE MORE TOWNS LIKE THIS.

SO... YOU'RE ALL ALONE?
TRAVELING, I MEAN.
WHAT ABOUT YOUR--
THEY'RE DEAD.
OH.
MY PARENTS ARE GONE, TOO.
WELL, I MEAN, THEY'RE STILL ALIVE.
THEY LEFT ME WITH MY GRAMPS AND AUNT NIFRAIN WHEN I WAS SMALL.
GONE TO LIVE OFF THE LAND. OR SOMETHING.
I WOULD'VE SLOWED 'EM DOWN.

HARD LUCK.
SOMETIMES I DREAM ABOUT SEEING THEM AGAIN...
AND PUNCHING THEM IN THEIR FACES.
AHHH...
SO, WHAT'S UP NORTH?
WHAT?
YOU'RE FROM THE GREATMIRE, AREN'T YOU?
THOSE LOOKED LIKE SOUTH JUNGLE CLOTHES YOU WERE WEARING WHEN WE FOUND YOU.
THAT FAR SOUTH, THERE'S ONLY ONE DIRECTION TO GO.
PRETTY GOOD GUESS.
WELL...
LIKE YOU SAID, WE'RE PRETTY ISOLATED OUT HERE.
GOTTA GET MY ADVEN-TURES IN HOWEVER I CAN.
SWORD & HAMMER

YOU STUDY MAPS?
WELL, I--
WHOA...
WATCH IT!
KRSHHH!
WHAT THE HELL?!

...
EVERYONE...
EVERYONE...
PROCEED QUICKLY AND CALMLY TO THE SQUARE WITH YOUR CONTRIBUTIONS.
PLEASE DON'T PANIC.

STEP RIGHT UP!
THAT'S RIGHT, FRIENDS!

MONEY'S GOOD.
FOOD'S EVEN BETTER!
AHAHAHAHA!

AND IF I LIKE WHAT YA GIVE ME...
MAYBE I WON'T TOSS YER PUNY LITTLE MAYOR--
WUHUHUH...!
...TO THE OTHER SIDE OF THE CONTINENT.

MOOOOOOO!
JAIME!
GET OVER 'ERE AND HELP WITH THIS!
YOU KNOW YOUR WAY BACK TO THE CLINIC?
...
YEAH, SURE..

A TRIBUTE TO OUR SUPERIORS.

"WE GET ROGUES EVERY FEW WEEKS OR SO."
"THEY TRAVEL FROM TOWN TO TOWN."
"ASKING FOR HANDOUTS..."
"...AND TAKING WHAT IS REFUSED TO THEM."
KSSHHHHH
"WE CAN BEAT OFF THE NORMAL ONES..."
"BUT NOT THIS KIND."
HE'S...
A PARASAI.

"FUNNY, ISN'T IT?"
"IN GREATER, MORE PROSPEROUS PARTS OF ROJARDIN..."
"PARASAI WOULD BE PROTECTING PEOPLE FROM THIS SORT OF THING."
"BUT NOT OUT HERE."
"THE CONFEDERACY DOESN'T CARE ABOUT THE LIKES OF US."
"HERE, PARASAI ARE ONLY TROUBLE."
WE DON'T WELCOME THEM HERE.
NOT EVER.
HOW DID YOU KNOW?

"YOUR BLOOD."
"YOU'RE NOT THE FIRST ROGUE PARASAI I'VE PATCHED UP, YOU KNOW."
SIGH
IT'S NOT IN ME TO TURN A PATIENT OUT.
"YOU'LL STAY UNTIL YOUR WOUNDS HAVE HEALED."
"AND THEN YOU'LL BE ON YOUR WAY."
FINE.
WASN'T PLANNING ON STAYING, ANYWAY.
END CHAPTER ONE

ABBIE!

ABBIE...
LISTEN TO ME...
HEY!

WHATCHA THINKIN' ABOUT?
NOTHING.
JUST THE WEATHER.
WHAT'S THIS?
YOU WERE ASKING ME ABOUT MAPS, REMEMBER?
TOOK ME A WHILE TO DIG THESE OUT, BUT...
SUSAN
GLADIOLUS
THEY'RE NOT HARD TO READ.

WHAT'S HARD IS GETTING YOUR BEARINGS ONCE YOU'RE OUT THERE.
DO YOU HAVE A COMPASS? AND ALMANAC?
SHAKE
WELL, THERE ARE OTHER WAYS.
I COULD TEACH YOU, IF YOU WANT?
YEAH.
ONLY IF IT WON'T TAKE LONG.
I SHOULD BE ON MY WAY SOON.

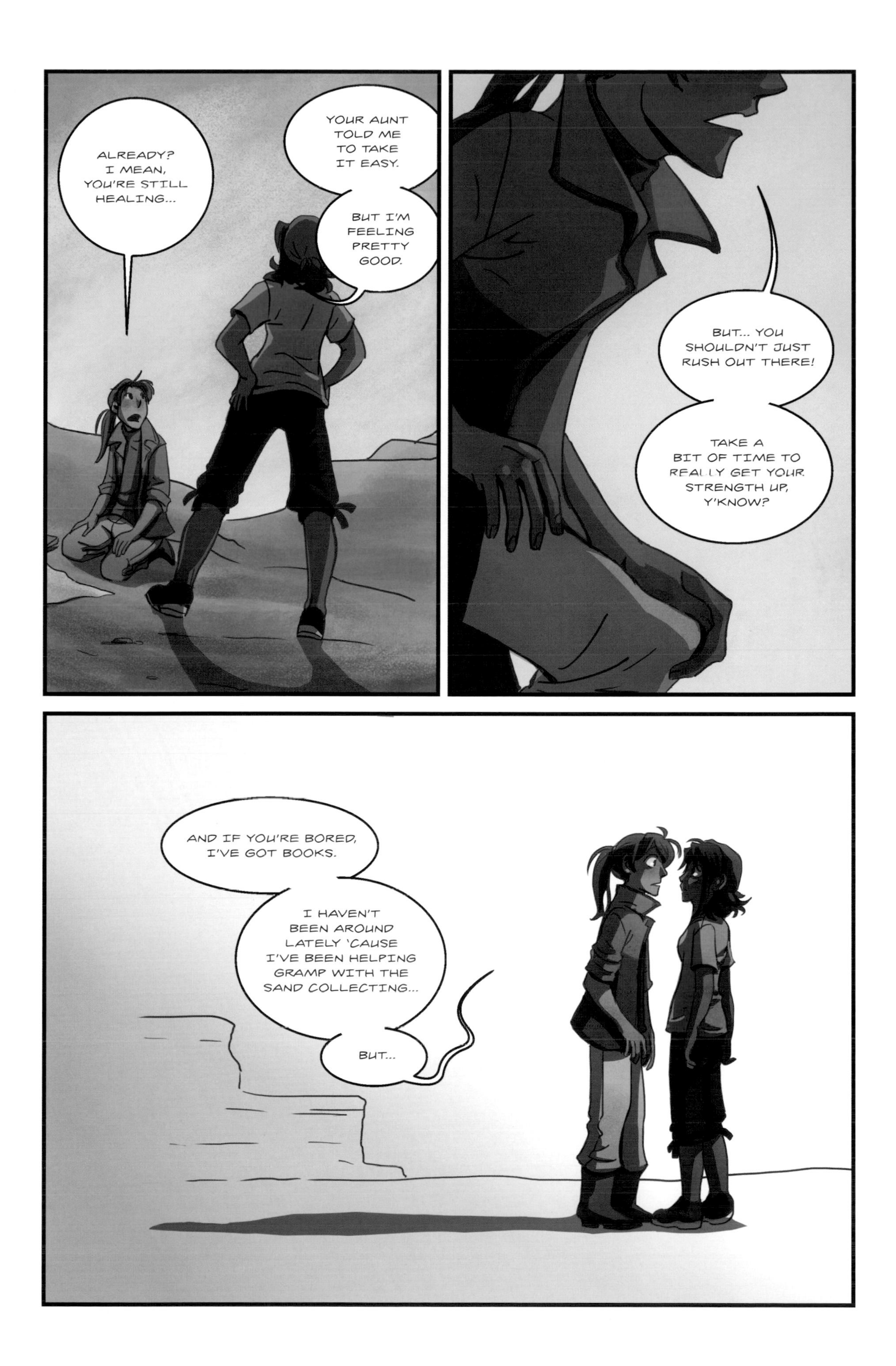
ALREADY? I MEAN, YOU'RE STILL HEALING...
YOUR AUNT TOLD ME TO TAKE IT EASY.
BUT I'M FEELING PRETTY GOOD.
BUT... YOU SHOULDN'T JUST RUSH OUT THERE!
TAKE A BIT OF TIME TO REALLY GET YOUR STRENGTH UP, Y'KNOW?
AND IF YOU'RE BORED, I'VE GOT BOOKS.
I HAVEN'T BEEN AROUND LATELY 'CAUSE I'VE BEEN HELPING GRAMP WITH THE SAND COLLECTING...
BUT...

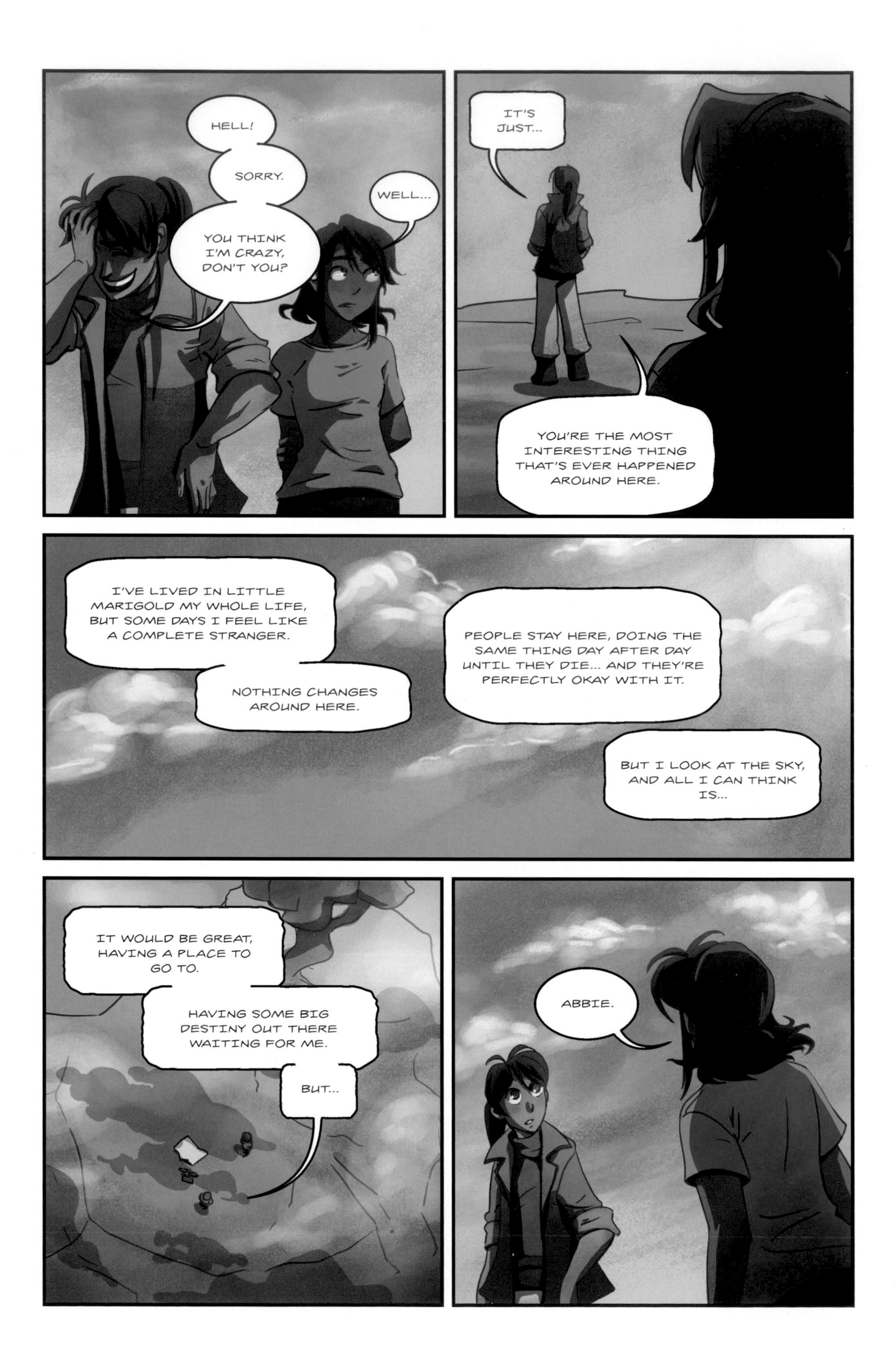
HELL!
SORRY.
YOU THINK I'M CRAZY, DON'T YOU?
WELL...
IT'S JUST...
YOU'RE THE MOST INTERESTING THING THAT'S EVER HAPPENED AROUND HERE.
I'VE LIVED IN LITTLE MARIGOLD MY WHOLE LIFE, BUT SOME DAYS I FEEL LIKE A COMPLETE STRANGER.
NOTHING CHANGES AROUND HERE.
PEOPLE STAY HERE, DOING THE SAME THING DAY AFTER DAY UNTIL THEY DIE... AND THEY'RE PERFECTLY OKAY WITH IT.
BUT I LOOK AT THE SKY, AND ALL I CAN THINK IS...
IT WOULD BE GREAT, HAVING A PLACE TO GO TO.
HAVING SOME BIG DESTINY OUT THERE WAITING FOR ME.
BUT...
ABBIE.

WHAT?
MY NAME. I'M ABBIE.
BUT, UH, YEAH, MAPS.
I COULD STILL TEACH YOU.
IT WON'T TAKE LONG.
JUST STEER CLEAR OF SANDSTORMS, AND YOU'LL BE FINE.

THWACK
IF YOU'VE GOT SO MUCH FREE TIME, JAIME...
YOU CAN HELP ME CATALOG THE HERB STORE.
DUTY CALLS.
WHY DON'T YOU GET SOME EXERCISE? TAKE SOME FOOD TO MY FATHER.
HE'S IN THE GLASS SHOP. JAIME SHOWED YOU WHERE, RIGHT?
YEAH.

HEL...
LO?

WHATCHA GOT THERE?

OH, I--
AHHH!
TWENTY SEVERED TONGUES I'M SOSORRRRR--
OOH, LUNCH!

GLADIOLI GLASS.
A LOCAL SPECIALTY, YOU COULD SAY.
STRONGER THAN STONE.
TRICKY TO WORK, THOUGH, SO I SAVE IT FOR SPECIAL THINGS.
OOH. A PICKLE.
IT... IT REMINDED ME OF...
HMM?
SOMEONE I KNEW, ONCE.
MADE THAT FOR MY WIFE.
SHE ALWAYS LOVED MARIGOLDS.
ANYWAY, YOU'RE LOOKIN' FIT.
BUT I GUESS THERE AIN'T MUCH KEEPS YOU DOWN FOR LONG, HRM?
YOU... NIFRAIN TOLD YOU.
YEEEEP.

...
DOES IT BOTHER YOU?
WHO, ME? PUH! WHAT FOR?
SEEMS LIKE YOU GOT A GOOD HEAD ON YOUR SHOULDERS.
CAN'T NAVIGATE WORTH SPIT, BUT EVERYONE'S GOT THEIR FOIBLES.
THANKS...
ANY CASE, I DON'T GOT NOTHIN' 'GAINST YA.
I KNEW SOME PARASAI. SERVED ALONGSIDE 'EM, EVEN!
REALLY?
MMF. IN THE REGULARS. THAT WAS YEARS AGO, THOUGH. DIFFERENT DAY.
LITTLE MARIGOLD WAS ALIVE, THEN.
CAN'T SAY THE SAME NOW.

"THIS TOWN IS LOSIN' THE LIFE THAT BROUGHT US HERE, LITTLE BY LITTLE."

"DUNNO HOW MUCH IT'S GOT LEFT TO GIVE."

IS THAT WHY JAIME'S PARENTS LEFT?

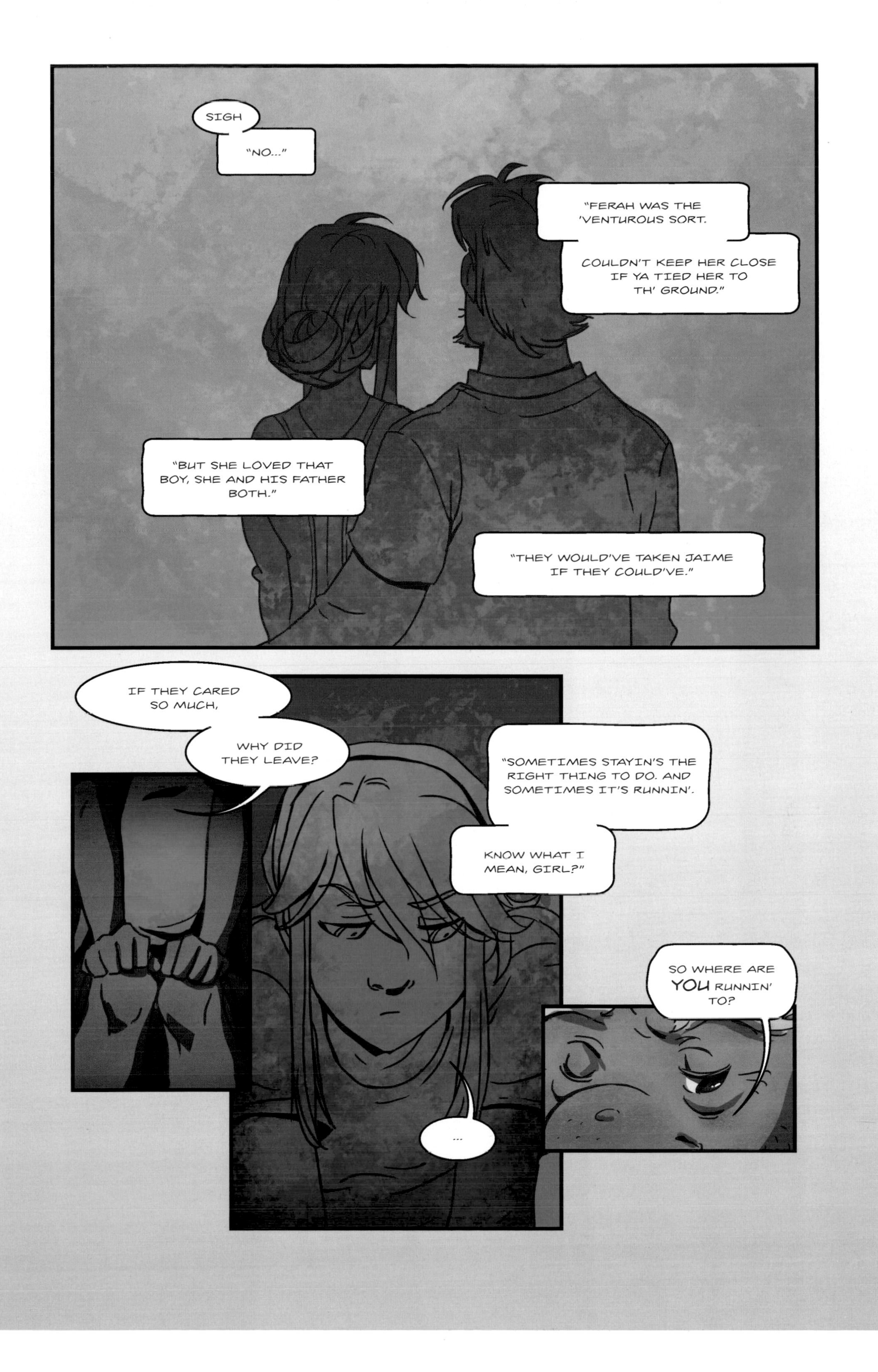
SIGH
"NO..."
"FERAH WAS THE 'VENTUROUS SORT.
COULDN'T KEEP HER CLOSE IF YA TIED HER TO TH' GROUND."
"BUT SHE LOVED THAT BOY, SHE AND HIS FATHER BOTH."
"THEY WOULD'VE TAKEN JAIME IF THEY COULD'VE."
IF THEY CARED SO MUCH,
WHY DID THEY LEAVE?
"SOMETIMES STAYIN'S THE RIGHT THING TO DO. AND SOMETIMES IT'S RUNNIN'.
KNOW WHAT I MEAN, GIRL?"
...
SO WHERE ARE YOU RUNNIN' TO?

I'M NOT SURE ANYMORE.
I JUST NEED...
TO FIND PERSPECTIVE...
DING DING DING DING
DING DING DING DING
DING DING DING DING DING
DING DING DING DING
ROGUES AGAIN?
...THE FOUR.
WHAT?
DIFFERENT RINGS FOR DIFFERENT WARNINGS.
FOUR SETS OF FOUR IS...
GET BACK TO THE CLINIC.
DING DING DING
GO ON! AND KEEP TO THE BACK ROADS!
DING DING DING DING
DING DING DING

TCH.
WHY DON'T YOU JUST POISON THEM WITH THOSE THINGS, AUNTIE?
I WOULD, IF I COULD BE SURE THEY'D USE THEM.
MOST LIKELY THEY JUST SELL THEM FOR COIN.
YOU COULD OFFER THEM PIGEON SOUP...
HAHA!
WAS THAT A JOKE?!
SHE MADE A JOKE!
AUNTIE, I DECLARE OUR PATIENT FULLY
RECOVERED!
ALL RIGHT, YOU, GET OUT THERE.
I'LL TAKE IT--
NOT YOU.

THIS ISN'T YOUR BUSINESS.
STAY HERE AND DON'T TOUCH ANYTHING.
CLICK
FFF.
I WASN'T GONNA HELP, ANYWAY...
HOME FEELS FARTHER AWAY THE CLOSER WE GET.
HUH, MOM...?

HIC
HIC
UWEHHHH..
WEH
WEH
WEHHHEHHH!
AW, YEAH...
I LOVE THIS TOWN!

D-DO YOU LIKE IT?
IT TASTES LIKE A BOILED POTATO SACK!
O... OH...
BUT BEGGARS CAN'T BE CHOOSERS, RIGHT?!
LITTLE MARIGOLD'S NOTHIN' BUT A DRIED UP HOLE IN THE GROUND.
BUT Y'VE MANAGED TO HOLD ON TO THOSE QUAINT DESERT CHARMS.
THAT'S 'CAUSE YOU KNOW YOUR PLACE.
RIGHT, GUYS?
YEAH!
CHIN UP, KID.
IT AIN'T SO BAD.

YOUR PARENTS SHOULDA TOLD YOU THIS...
EVERYONE PAYS THEIR DUES, KID. THE WEAK FEED THE STRONG.
IT'S CRUEL, SURE, BUT THAT'S WHAT NATURE IS.
TCH.
THERE'S NOTHING NATURAL ABOUT THIS.
SHUT UP!
THWAP!
AND WHAT'RE YOU TWO WHISPERIN' ABOUT?

HEY, I'M TEACHING THINGS!
YOU TWO THINK YOU'RE TOO GOOD FOR TEACHIN', HUH?

NO.

ALWAYS GIVIN' US THE SAME OLD GOAT PISS, DOC.
YOU THINK IT'S VALU-ABLE JUST 'CAUSE IT'S IN A FANCY BOTTLE?
THAT'S OINTMENT FOR SCORPION CACTUS STINGS. AN APOTHECARY WILL PAY GOOD MONEY FOR--
GOOD MONEY?
WHO'M I GONNA SELL TO OUT HERE, HUH?!
THIS IS THE BIGGEST TOWNLET IN THIS WHOLE DAMN DESERT.
AND YOU'RE POORER THAN FERGUS'S GRAMMAR!
HE AIN'T PLAYIN'!
'M THINKING SHE'S HOLDIN' OUT ON US. WHAT DO YOU GUYS THINK?
RECKON YER RIGHT, BOSS.

LET'S TAKE A LOOK THEN, EH?
STOP!
DON'T YOU DARE!
IT'S A CLINIC, NOT A CORNER STORE!
HEH. NOW I KNOW YOU'RE HOLDIN' OUT.
WHAM!

COO!
SSSSSS
CRASH!
PLOP
HEY. LOOKS LIKE THEY'RE HIDING SOMETHIN' IN HERE!
ICE
AW, C'MON!

UMPH!

EHEHEHE...
LOOKIE WHAT WE FOOOUND!

AND WHADDAYA KNOW! DOC, I'M SURPRISED AT YOU.
WELL, LET'S SEE WHAT YOU'VE BEEN HIDING.
NO!
GIVE IT BACK!

ASHES! I SHOULDA KNOWN.
CRACK!
YOU'RE COMPLETELY USELESS, DOC.
Y'KNOW THAT?

ABBIE, ARE YOU HURT?

IT'S ASH...
THAT WAS A CREMATION URN...
THE POOR THING.
THAT'S TOO MUCH.
YOU'VE GONE TOO FAR...
UH...YOU GUYS...
SHE'S OUR GUEST!
YOU THINK I CARE?
NO RESPECT FOR THE DEAD!
SHE'S JUST A KID!
WHAT GIVES YOU THE RIGHT?!
HEY SHUT UP!!

WHAT GIVES ME THE RIGHT...
SSSZZZZ
HSOOOOWS
THIS!

"POWER!"
"IT'S ALWAYS BEEN THIS WAY."
"THE DEVAS GAVE US THIS STRENGTH..."
"TO CREATE AND DESTROY..."
"TO LEAD AND CONQUER!"
"AS A PARASAI THIS POWER IS MY RIGHT..."
"AND MY BURDEN."
YOU'RE NO PARASAI.

"WUH?"
YOU HEARD ME.
REAL PARASAI KEEP PEOPLE SAFE.
"THEY HELP AND DEFEND THE WEAK AGAINST THIEVES AND MURDERERS..."
"...LIKE YOU.
YOU'RE NO REAL PARASAI."
!!
YOU'RE JUST A THUG AND A COWARD!

THAT SO, KID?
AND WHAT'S A HICK LIKE YOU KNOW ABOUT REAL PARASAI?
LOOK AROUND YOU.
YOU SEE ANYTHING WORTH PROTECTING AROUND HERE?
ALL I SEE IS A BUNCH OF SNIVELING SHEEP THAT CAN'T WAIT TO BE SHEARED.
BUT AT LEAST THOSE SHEEP HAVE THE SENSE TO KEEP THEIR MOUTHS SHUT.

STOP!
HAVE YOU LOST IT?!
RELAX, OLD MAN!
I'VE GOT FULL CONTROL.
THIS THING'S LIKE AN EXTENSION OF MY BODY.
BUT I HAVE BEEN KNOWN TO SLIP NOW AND THEN...
YOU KNOW THE BIG DIFFERENCE BETWEEN YOU AND ME? SCIENCE.
THE LIVING BODY IS A WONDER, KID. WE'RE NOTHING BUT SACKS OF MEAT AND BONE, AND WITH AIR AND JUST A FEW ELECTRIC PULSES, WE'RE ABLE TO SPEAK, THINK, AND REASON. BUT SOME OF US GOT MORE GOING ON IN THOSE PULSES THAN OTHERS, Y'KNOW?
MORE ENERGY FLOWING, MORE INFORMATION FLYIN'. YOU THINK YOU'RE SOMETHIN' WITH THAT BIG MOUTH OF YOURS...
BUT YOU AIN'T GOT A FRACTION OF THE POWER PARASAI LIKE ME ARE BORN WITH.
KNOW WHAT I'M SAYIN, KID?

STOP.

HA HA
OH, I'M SORRY.
ARE WE UPSETTING YOU?
HA HA
HA HA
HA HA
HA HA
EHEHE
LOOK IT 'ER!
GO ON...
RUN
CRY
TO
YER
MAMAAA
RUN TO MAMA!
MAMA MAMA MAMA
OR WE'LL MAKE YA RUN...
TNK
TNG
SHNG
TNK
YA
LI'L
MAMA'S
GIRL
...

OHOHOO...
I'LL MAKE YA RUN...
GET 'ER, DEREK!

RUN
TO
MAMA...

LEAVE 'ER!
JAIME!
TAKE A SEAT, FRIEND!

SZZZZT!
"NOW, JUST CALM DOWN."
I DIDN'T WANNA GO THIS FAR...
BUT YA FORCED MY HAND.
IT'S JUST BUSINESS, Y'KNOW? SO--

KRSSHH!
UNGHHH...
MY MOTHER'S DEAD, ASSHOLE

NO WAY...
SHE'S LIKE...
THE BOSS!

CRAAACK!
WSZZZN

.ZZZZ
ZZZ!

KABOOM

pnk
KRSH!
SHOOM

WHAT IS THIS?!

SH
KRSSHH
KRACK
SHHHK
MAYOR...
I'M DISAPPOINTED IN YOU.
HIRING A PARASAI WHILE I WAS OUT OF TOWN?!
SH
SH
SHE
SHE'S NOT...
NO ONE'S PAYING ME ANYTHING.

WHAT?!
SNAP
SHK
HEH, ANOTHER ROGUE, THEN!
NO...
SSZZZ
I'M NOT LIKE YOU.

THEN WHAT IS IT, HUH?! 'CAUSE I KNOW THE PEOPLE OF LITTLE MARIGOLD...
THEY HATE EVERYTHING TO DO WITH DIGNITY...
STRENGTH...
POWER!
AND PARASAI... THEY **HATE** PARASAI MOST OF ALL.
SO WHY DEFEND THEM? YOU SOME SORT OF DO-GOODER?
YOU GOT A SOFT SPOT FOR THE WEAK AND PATHETIC?

I'M NOT DOING IT FOR THEM.
I'M DOING IT BECAUSE YOU
PISSED
ME
OFF!

WHACK
WHAT... SORT OF POWER... IS THIS...
MY AERO... CAN CUT THROUGH STONE!
IT CAN CUT ANYTHING!
WHO ARE YOU...

WHAT ARE YOU?!
I'M...
...STRONGER THAN YOU, CLEARLY!

END CHAPTER TWO

WOW! CAN YOU BELIEVE THAT?
INCREDIBLE!
I SAW THOSE APPLES LIFT UP--
THEY BECAME HARD AS STONE!
AND THAT WHEEL--
SO SHE'S LIKE THEM?
SHE'S A PARASAI?
IN OUR TOWN?
HOW DID SHE GET HERE?
SHE'S THAT GIRL IMAN AND HIS BOY FOUND OUT ON THE DUNES...
THEY BROUGHT HER HERE?!
WHAT DOES SHE WANT?

WE ARE...GRATEFUL FOR YOUR ACTIONS AGAINST THE FOUR.
WE HOPE THAT THIS MEAGER GIFT IS A SATISFACTORY SHOW OF OUR APPRECIATION.
BUT... I DON'T...
PLEASE, TAKE IT AND BE...
AND BE ON YOUR WAY.

WE'RE A HUMBLE PEOPLE HERE. WE KNOW OUR PLACE IN THE WORLD...
AND WE HAVE NO TROUBLE WITH PAYING WHAT'S DUE TO THOSE WHO ARE BETTER.
ALL WE ASK IS TO LIVE OUR LIVES IN PEACE.
AND...
AND YOUR PRESENCE HERE WILL ONLY DISRUPT THAT PEACE, YOU SEE?
YEAH... I SEE.
WAIT!
WHA--!

ABBIE, WHAT YOU DID--THAT WAS...
INCREDIBLE!
WE'VE NEVER BEEN ABLE TO STAND UP TO THOSE GUYS.
BUT YOU... YOU TOOK OUT THE WHOLE GANG ALL ON YOUR OWN!
STAY.
STAY **HERE**, IN LITTLE MARIGOLD!
NOW, JAIME, PLEASE, WE'RE A **GENTLE** PEOPLE. IT WOULD BE IMPRUDENT TO ALLOW THIS... THIS CREATURE TO REMAIN AMONG US.
THINK OF THE DESTRUCTION SHE CAUSED. SHE'LL ONLY ATTRACT MORE TROUBLE FOR US IN THE END...
DON'T YOU THINK?
WHAT?!
NO, I DON'T THINK THAT AT **ALL**!
HE'S RIGHT.

W-WAIT! ABBIE, WE--
I NEVER MEANT TO COME HERE ANYWAY, YOU KNOW.
I'VE GOT A LONG WAY TO GO...
AND YOU'RE ALL WASTING MY TIME.
WHY ARE YOU CHASING HER OFF?!
THINK OF THE GOOD SHE COULD DO HERE!
WE NEED HER. LITTLE MARIGOLD NEEDS HER!
I KNOW WHAT THAT GIRL DID LOOKS LIKE VALOR TO YOU...
BUT THERE'S NO SUCH THING OUT HERE.
THERE'S ONLY SURVIVAL.
HOW IS THIS SURVIVAL?!
THEY TAKE OUR MONEY, OUR FOOD, AND WE JUST LET THEM!
WE DROP IT AT THEIR FEET AND BEG THEM TO TAKE MORE,
LIKE COWARDS!
COWARDS?
YOU THINK WHAT WE DO IS COWARDLY?

OUR PEOPLE HAVE TRIED TO FIGHT BACK AGAINST ROGUES IN THE PAST.
WE HAVE STOOD UP TO THEM, DOWN TO A MAN.
"BUT WE ARE NOT PARASAI, JAIME."
"THEY CALL US MISMA IN THE CAPITAL."
"THE SAME."
"UNCHANGED, ORDINARY, WEAK."
"WE ARE SIMPLY NO MATCH FOR THEIR KIND."
IT IS NOT COWARDLY.
IT IS NATURE!

AND DO YOU THINK NATURE INTENDS TO JUST WIPE LITTLE MARIGOLD FROM THE EARTH?
AFTER ALL WE'VE SUFFERED...
ARE WE GOING TO LET CRIMINALS TAKE WHAT FEW TREASURES WE HAVE LEFT?
I WILL GIVE THEM WHATEVER THEY ASK IF IT MEANS KEEPING PEACE HERE.
TREASURES CAN BE REMADE. LIVES CANNOT.
YOU'D DO WELL TO TEACH YOUR GRANDSON, IMAN.

WHERE IS SHE?!
NOT HERE. GONE--
ABBIE!

shhk
FOOM
FOOM

ABBIE!
ABBIE, WAIT UP!
ABBIE!
...
I CAN'T STAY HERE, JAIME.
I KNOW.
N... NEITHER CAN I.
LET ME COME WITH YOU.
PLEASE.

...
NO.
ABBIE--
HELL NO!
ARE YOU INSANE?!
WE JUST MET!
YOU'VE BEEN STAYIN' AT MY PLACE FOR TWO WEEKS!
YOU... YOU DON'T EVEN KNOW WHERE I'M HEADED!
WELL? WHERE ARE YOU HEADED?
TO THE MAINLAND, RIGHT?!
...NONE OF YOUR BUSINESS.
JUST LET ME GO WITH YOU AS FAR AS--
WHAT ABOUT YOUR FAMILY?
ARE YOU JUST GONNA UP AND DITCH THEM--
MY FAMILY DOESN'T LIVE HERE ANYMORE, ABBIE!
MY FAMILY DITCHED ME.
A LONG TIME AGO.
IT'S JUST... NOT FAIR.

"NOT TO ME, NOT TO GRAMP OR NIFRAIN."
"THEY'VE BEEN TAKING CARE OF ME FOR THE LAST ELEVEN YEARS."
"AND THEY NEVER COMPLAINED, Y'KNOW?"
"THEY'VE NEVER EVEN BADMOUTHED MY FOLKS."
"MY MOM AND DAD, WHO JUST DROPPED ME ON THEIR DOORSTEP AND NEVER LOOKED BACK."
"I'M TIRED OF BEING A BURDEN."
"THE LEAST I CAN DO FOR THEM..."
"...IS MAKE MY WAY IN THE WORLD."
"FIND SOMETHING TO LIVE FOR."
I...
I CAN'T COOK WELL, BUT I'LL TRY.

I CAN IDENTIFY ALL TYPES OF PLANTS AND ANIMALS...
SO YOU WON'T HAVE TO WORRY ABOUT GETTING STUNG OR POISONED.
AND... AND IF THINGS GET BORING, I CAN TELL JOKES.
AND I KNOW TONS OF STORIES.
I CAN KEEP YOU COMPANY, JUST...
PLEASE, JUST...
SIGH
YOUR JOKES ARE TERRIBLE, THOUGH.
WELL?
YOU PROBABLY WANT TO GRAB A CHANGE OF CLOTHES OR SOME-THIN', RIGHT?

GO AWAY.
JAIME...
I'M GOING, AUNTIE.
...
YOUR MOTHER COULD NEVER SIT STILL, EITHER.
BUT THEN, YOU ALREADY KNOW THAT.
I SAW A RAKUNA THE DAY SHE LEFT FOR THE LAST TIME.
YOU KNOW WHY THEY'RE CALLED "RAKUNA," RIGHT?

"THEY'RE THE SERVANTS OF RAKU, DEVA OF LONG JOURNEYS."
"AND DIFFICULT TIMES."
"I WAS NEVER RELIGIOUS, BUT..."
"THE IMAGE OF THAT ANIMAL, WATCHING ME FROM THE HILL..."
"HAS ALWAYS STAYED IN MY MIND."
WHEN YOU FIRST CAME HERE, I WAS ANGRY.
YOUR MOTHER WAS ALWAYS SO INDEPENDENT AND RASH, EVEN WHEN WE WERE KIDS.
LEAVING HER ONLY CHILD WAS SOMETHING SHE'D DO...
JUST LIKE SHE LEFT ME AND DAD.
"MOSTLY I WAS ANGRY WITH MYSELF."
"FOR GIVING UP ON HER."
"FOR NOT CONVINCING HER TO STAY."

BUT I WOULD REMEMBER THE RAKUNA.
AND, OVER TIME, I REALIZED IT WOULDN'T HAVE MADE A DIFFERENCE.
"FERAH WAS ALWAYS MEANT FOR A BIGGER LIFE.
WE CAN'T KEEP EVERY-THING THE WAY WE WANT IT TO BE FOREVER.
IT'S JUST THE WAY IT IS."
"WE CAN'T FIGHT NATURE."
"AND YOU, JAIME...
YOU ARE YOUR MOTHER'S SON."

AUNTIE...
I--
THWAP
YOU WEREN'T PLANNING TO LEAVE WITHOUT SAYING GOODBYE TO YOUR GRANDFATHER, SURELY?
N-NO...
GRAMP?
I... I GOT SOMETHING TO SAY.
I'M--
I KNOW!
I'M OLD. I AIN'T BLIND.
C'MERE.
BEEN WAITIN' TO GIVE THIS TO YOU.
HAD THAT SINCE I WAS A YOUNG MAN.
JOURNEYS RUN IN THE FAMILY, Y'KNOW?

YEAH...
AUNTIE TOLD ME.
WHERE'S THE GIRL?
WAITING FOR ME.
I THINK...
C'MON. I GOT SOMETHIN' FOR HER TOO.
SHHHFF
AIN'T MUCH, BUT IT'S STURDY.
Y' REMEMBER WHAT I TOLDJA 'BOUT GLADIOLI GLASS, EH?
THANK YOU.

I'M SORRY, GRAMP, AUNTIE.
LEAVING LIKE THIS.
I JUST--
Y'AINT GOT NOTHIN' TO APOLOGIZE FOR, BOY.
IT'S IN SOME'S NATURE TO STAY, AND IN SOME'S TO RUN.
AIN'T THAT RIGHT, GIRL?
...
SWIPE
SWIPE
WEAR THIS.
AUNTIE, WHY ARE YOU BEING SO NICE?
CONSIDER IT INCENTIVE FOR TAKING CARE OF YOU.
JEEZ, THANKS.
CAN I GIVE YOU SOME ADVICE?

WHAT'RE YOU GUYS TALKTN' ABOUT?
UH... NOTHING.
THE WEATHER.
HAHA.
YOU'RE PRETTY LAME AT LYING, Y'KNOW?
IT'S LATE.
SURE YOU WANT TO SET OFF RIGHT NOW?
WHY NOT WAIT TILL MORNING?
IT'LL BE BURNIN' UP IN THE MORNING.
BESIDES, IT'S A CLEAR NIGHT.
WE'LL BE ABLE TO SEE FOR HOURS YET.

SERIOUSLY, THOUGH.
WHAT DID SHE SAY?
SHE TOLD ME TO TRUST YOU.

END CHAPTER THREE

www.insightcomics.com

Find us on Facebook: www.facebook.com/InsightEditionsComics
Follow us on Twitter: @InsightComics
Follow us on Instagram: Insight_Comics

Published by Insight Editions, San Rafael, California, in 2017.

Library of Congress Cataloging-in-Publication Data available.

ISBN: 978-1-68383-004-7

Publisher: Raoul Goff
Executive Editor: Vanessa Lopez
Art Director: Chrissy Kwasnik
Managing Editor: Alan Kaplan
Senior Editor: Mark Irwin
Production Editor: Elaine Ou
Production Manager: Alix Nicholaeff

Insight Editions, in association with Roots of Peace, will plant two trees for each tree used in the manufacturing of this book. Roots of Peace is an internationally renowned humanitarian organization dedicated to eradicating land mines worldwide and converting war-torn lands into productive farms and wildlife habitats. Roots of Peace will plant two million fruit and nut trees in Afghanistan and provide farmers there with the skills and support necessary for sustainable land use.

Manufactured in China by Insight Editions

10 9 8 7 6 5 4 3 2